you

ruined

me

by Sabre Rose

ALL RIGHTS RESERVED BY THE AUTHOR
Published by Sabre Rose

© 2021 Sabre Rose
Digital Edition © 2018 Sabre Rose

This book is a work of fiction.
Any resemblance to actual events, any person living or deceased is entirely coincidental. Any references to real places or events are used fictitiously. All characters and storylines are products of the author's imagination.

No part of this book may be reproduced, re-sold, or transmitted electronically or otherwise, without express written permission from the author, except in the case of brief quotations embodied in critical reviews and certain other non-commercial uses permitted by copyright.

For more information about the author visit:
www.sabreroseauthor.com

ISBN: 9798748330459

You knew me but I didn't know you.

To me you were a stranger.
A random person in the crowd.
No one.

If I could go back, if I knew what I know now, I would have run.

But I can't go back.

And I didn't know better.

Not then.

I didn't know you would ruin me.

Ruin me with lies.

With lust.

With longing.

Just look at me now in this world without you.

I have nothing.

This is not a love story.

It is a story of obsession.

*This story contains dark scenes of a sexual nature.
Reader discretion is advised.*

one

It was a chance meeting. Or so I thought at the time. It seemed so cliché, how we met. Something that only happened in books or movies. Fantasy not reality. If I could go back, if I knew what I know now, I would have run. I would have taken one look at your lazy smile, at your lips that were a shade darker than most, at your pale skin and tousled dark hair, and I would have run.

But I can't go back.

And I didn't know better.

Not then.

I didn't know you would ruin me.

I was at the movies with Jess. She begged me to go. Even though it wasn't a movie I was interested in, I went anyway because that's what friends do. And I had nothing else on. Dad was at home, doing what he did every night. Sitting on the couch, whiskey glass in hand, staring blankly at the television as it attempted to amuse him. It was rarely successful.

Jess liked cliché movies. She liked that they were predictable, that the good guys always won. I didn't. But I should have. There is something to be said when evil is punished and goodness is rewarded.

It's the way it should be.

But it's not the way the world is.

We were waiting in line to buy tickets and arguing about ice cream. She liked the crunch of the chocolate-covered topping. I didn't. She wanted vanilla. I wanted boysenberry. It seemed important at the time.

So distracted was I by our argument, I never noticed you watching. I never noticed the way your eyes narrowed with recognition.

You knew me but I didn't know you.

To me you were a stranger.

A random person in the crowd.

No one.

It wasn't until you caught me that I saw you. One minute I was standing in line and the next I was falling into you. I didn't know that you were the one who made me fall. That you saw me and knew who I was. That you planned it all.

Later, I would look back and imagine telling our children how we met. It was silly, I know, but I liked to imagine. I liked to think of a world where chance meetings turned into love. We would laugh as we recalled the story. Our eyes would shine over the heads of our children. We would smile. Our hair would be speckled with grey. You would kiss my cheek.

We would be happy.

Those around us chuckled when I stumbled. But you saved me. Colour flooded my cheeks as I found myself clutching onto you, my head buried in your chest.

You smelled of rain and of smoke and of something sharp.

You helped me to my feet, depositing me back beside Jess. "Are you alright?"

Jess laughed. "Don't mind her. She's as clumsy as they come."

It was a lie but you didn't know that. You didn't know the only reason Jess said it was because she thought you were attractive. And you were. Dressed in a leather jacket with rough patches on the elbows, you looked at me and smiled. And it was in that moment I decided I would not take the backseat. Jess wanted you but fate had delivered me into your lap. Almost literally.

"I'm fine." That was the masterpiece of a reply I came up with. Jess was the bold one. Jess was the one with the witty replies and battering lashes.

You hovered by my side as though you were afraid I might fall again. "Are you sure?"

Jess grabbed my arm, tugging me forward as the line moved. "She's quite sure, thank you." She had decided to go for the 'blunt' option. Hard to get. This was the tact she took with most men she liked, and I knew she liked you by the tilt of her chin and the glint of mischief in her eyes.

But you didn't respond. You took your place behind me and every time I stole glances over my shoulder, I was met with the intensity of your gaze. Your eyes were heavy, as if you despised the world so much you couldn't stand to see it fully. I liked the way they fixed so solidly on me. You weren't afraid that I would notice you were watching. You wanted me to.

Once we had made our purchases, you approached the counter and requested tickets to the same movie. You didn't use its name. You didn't ask for recommendations. You looked the girl in the eye and asked for four tickets to the same movie as me. It was only then that I noticed the rest of your group. There were four of you. All male. All intent on seeing a different movie than the one you requested. They groaned and cursed. I didn't blame them. Their complaints echoed my own when Jess suggested it, but you held firm, your eyes sliding to mine, holding a question or a challenge. I wasn't sure which.

Jess grabbed my arm again, almost causing me to spill the overstuffed box of popcorn. I hated popcorn because I could never stop eating it. I hated it because it got caught in my teeth, because it was both salty and sweet, crunchy and soft. But I still ordered it. Maybe I was attracted to things I hated. Maybe that's why I noticed you. Subconsciously, I knew that one day I would hate you.

We sat in the middle of the theatre. Middle seats. Middle

row. It was tradition. I kept looking over my shoulder, waiting for you to appear. Jess noticed and elbowed me in the ribs. She was physical like that. Hitting and slapping, hugging and squeezing.

"You like him." She said it in a sing-song voice, as though we were thirteen again and she was taunting me.

"I do not." I spoke with none of the maturity my twenty-one years deserved and poked out my tongue.

Then I glanced over my shoulder again.

"Oh my god, you do!" Narrowing her eyes, Jess leaned in close. "I wonder if he's any good in bed? He looks like he could be. He looks fit. Lean." Her head cocked to the side. "Then again, you never can tell."

I ignored her and shoved a handful of popcorn into my mouth.

And then you walked in.

I promised myself I wouldn't look. You were nothing more than a stranger in a theatre who I would never see again, but all that fell by the wayside when you sat beside me.

You smiled and held out your hand. "Killian."

The proximity made it awkward to shake your offered greeting. "Sophie." My name was mumbled around popcorn. I swallowed. "What sort of a name is Killian?"

You lifted your eyebrows. "What sort of a name is Sophie?"

I shrugged, feeling the colour creep back into my cheeks. I didn't mean to sound so blunt, so accusing. I shrugged. "It's the name my parents gave me." After taking another handful of popcorn, I tilted the box your way and you buried your hand into the pile. Somehow it felt dangerous, naughty, as though we were caught in a forbidden act.

"Same," you said.

Then you sat back in your seat, placing one piece of popcorn in your mouth at a time and started to talk to your friends, dismissing me as nothing more than the girl you sat beside. Because that's all I thought I was. Your friends were still ribbing you about your movie choice. They had no idea it was because of me that you changed your mind.

If I had thought to notice them, I would have seen their groomed hair-styles, the stiffness of their collars and the expensive cut of their shirts. But I didn't notice any of these things because I only saw you.

I wanted to talk to you but my mind was blank. I couldn't think of one question to ask as the lights dimmed and the trailers started to roll. Not one amusing comment popped into my head. So instead, I tried to ignore you, even though I could feel the heat of your body next to mine.

During the movie, I stole glances at you. I noticed smudges of black across the ridge of your jaw and wanted to ask what they were from. I noticed your feet were placed on the back of the seat in front of you but you removed them when the usher walked past. And I noticed that your jeans were ripped and faded and covered in the same dark smudges that marred your face.

Your drink was in the cup holder closest to my seat and every time you reached for it, your arm brushed against mine. I wanted you to be doing it on purpose but I couldn't tell whether you were or not.

You ignored me, but the only thing I noticed was you.

Jess laughed loudly and I was jolted back to the movie. It was a romance of some sort. I didn't need to watch to know the plot. Boy meets girl. Boy and girl fall in love. Boy does something stupid. Girl is sad. Boy is sorry. They live happily ever after.

Jess was transfixed. She got emotionally invested in movies. She couldn't watch a sad scene without crying, just like she couldn't watch a funny scene without laughing. She even cried during television advertisements.

It was during the apology part, the part when the boy declared his undying love, when I felt the brush of your finger. It was faint at first and I thought I imagined it. But then it happened again.

Your hand was on the armrest. Mine was on my leg. They were close enough to touch, but not without effort. Your little finger stretched out to stroke mine. Such a small movement. So innocent. But it felt anything but. Your finger twisted to cover mine, linking us together in the smallest of ways.

I was on fire.

Alive.

I glanced over, but you were watching the movie. It was as

though you had no idea what you were doing. The flashing light of the screen illuminated your features, darkening the hollows under your eyes and sharpening the angles of your face. My heart raced. I was certain you would be able to feel the thud of my pulse through our entwined fingers.

The movie finished and the credits rolled. Red lights blinked, highlighting the steps of the theatre.

Your friend leaned forward. "What did you just make us watch? That was pure fucking rubbish." He rose to his feet.

I don't know when it happened but your touch was gone. My hand felt cold. I looked back up to find you staring at me, leaning forward, your hands grasping the armrests, ready to follow your friend. But instead you waited. For me.

"Did you like it?"

I glanced over at your friend's retreating back and mimicked his words. "It was pure fucking rubbish."

You stood and shrugged. "I didn't mind it."

Then you walked away.

And even though I barely knew you, even though I thought we were merely strangers who met at a movie, I felt the loss of you.

Jess tore my attention away by elbowing me. "So, what did you think? Did you like it?"

I smiled. "Sure did."

She stretched into the air, her top riding up her stomach. "Liar." She yawned. "But didn't you think it was sad when she stood there at the beginning, eating toast over the sink, all alone?"

"Why would that be sad?" I was genuinely confused.

"Never mind," Jess muttered. "I forgot you actually like being alone."

"Not all of the time."

"Most of it."

It was true. I worked. I ate dinner with my dad. I watched television in my room. I went to sleep. Loneliness didn't worry me. I was content to get lost in worlds that weren't my own. I wasn't always that way. Things were different after my sister left.

Not that she left voluntarily, but it sounds so much nicer than dead.

Even though Dad still had hope, even though for the police it was an unsolved case, I knew she was dead. She would have found her way back to me if she wasn't. Nothing would have stopped her.

I dumped the leftover popcorn in the bin and exited the theatre. And there you were, waiting for me, leaning against the wall, ankles crossed and your hands pressed into the pockets of your jeans. As I approached, you tipped forward and fell into step with me, phone in hand.

"Can I have your number?"

"Mine?"

Later, I wondered if you had seen the eagerness in my expression. Did you laugh at how easy it was? How quickly I fell?

Beside me, Jess groaned. "My god, Sophie. He's not asking for my number, is he?"

I flashed you a nervous smile, fumbling through my jacket pockets, searching for my phone. Then I realised I didn't need it and the creases of your mouth crept up. It had never happened to me before. I didn't attract attention. I took after my dad like that, even though, physically, I was the spitting image of my mother and my sister.

Pulling my hand out of my pocket, I told you my number and you tapped it into your phone.

"Thanks."

And then you were gone again. Only this time it didn't feel like loss.

Jess chuckled. "Sheesh, he's keen. A little strange, but keen."

"He was nice."

"Nice?" Jess shuddered. "Fuck nice."

My phone vibrated in my pocket. There was a message from you and with it came the first clue, though it never occurred to me at the time. At the time it was nothing. I didn't register. If I had, it would have set off alarm bells. But I doubt I would have listened. I was too taken with you. There were too many explanations, reasons, excuses. Too many things in my mind that made me blind to your intention.

Keying in the lock code, I pressed on the new message.

'It was nice to meet you Sophie Rush.'

two

My arms ached. My feet throbbed. I had been standing for eight hours. I stank of dough and cheese and pepperoni.

"You working tomorrow?" Caleb leaned against the wall, watching as I pulled my apron over my head. It was streaked with flour and tomato sauce.

"Weekend off."

"Want to hit the clubs tomorrow night?"

He asked me that every weekend and every weekend my answer was the same. The first time I said yes was the only time I said yes. It was a few months after my sister went missing and Caleb insisted on taking me out. He fed me something he called a tab and I spent the rest of my night caught in a nightmare where time both slowed down and sped up. Caleb talked about it as though it were legendary. All I wanted to do was forget. I ended up in bed with a stranger, Caleb in the next room, my mouth dry and foul, and my mind filled with shame.

"Think I'll just stay in."

Caleb rolled his eyes, crossed his arms over his chest and shook his head. "You are letting life pass you by, my dear girl."

I threw my apron into the pile at the back door, ready and waiting to be washed.

"No, I'm saving so I can have a life."

"Ah, yes." He grinned. "The great 'overseas experience'. When are you heading off again?"

Admittedly I had been going on about leaving for a while now. I think everyone just thought it was a dream. And it was, once. Phoebe and I used to talk about all the places we would visit. It was better than facing the drudgery of what my life would become if I stayed. She was going to come with me. We would travel the world. But deep down we knew it would never happen. We knew it was nothing more than wishful thinking. Then she was gone. And suddenly I needed to make it a reality. Dad thought it was a good idea too. He would have given me the money if he had it. Instead, I started working at the local pizza shop and I had been there ever since. Each week the money went into my bank account and each week I did my best to make sure it stayed there. Most of it anyway. Dad didn't work anymore. He couldn't. And there was only so much living you could do on a benefit.

I didn't answer Caleb and he didn't expect me to. He laughed, pulling himself away from the wall and walked off, his apron tossed over his shoulder. He always took it home and washed it himself. I didn't know why. "See you next week then."

"Looking forward to it," I replied dryly, letting my hair out of its ponytail and sighing in relief as it fell to my shoulders.

Caleb winked, glancing back over his shoulder. "Who wouldn't?"

* * *

The first thing I noticed as I pushed open our apartment door was the blare of the television, the fluorescent flashes of light that snuck around the corner from the lounge.

Dad was in his chair, head lolled to the side, gentle snores barely heard under the volume of the television.

I kissed the top of his head. "I'm home, Dad."

The snores stopped and he opened his eyes.

"Dinner's ready." I slid the pizza box onto the coffee table.

Dad sat forward. "Pineapple?"

"Of course."

Dad was a man of habit. He never varied from his choice in pizza toppings just like he never varied his daily routine. Apparently, before my mother died, he used to live. He had friends. He went hunting and fishing. Now his rifles and rods were locked away and forgotten.

"I'll just pop through the shower and then I'll join you." I tossed my jacket through the doorway to my bedroom. It landed on the bed then fell to the floor. "What are we watching?"

Dad looked up. "Coro," he mumbled around pizza. Friday night. The two-hour special. Dad was obsessed. Not obsessed enough to stay awake, but that was the fault of the nearly empty whiskey bottle sitting on the floor beside him.

I always felt better after a shower. Less greasy. Wiping my hand across the mirror, I smeared away the fog. I looked so much like her. Same eyes. Same hair. Same mouth, nose, ears. Same face. I knew that it pained Dad to look at me sometimes because I reminded him of her. I reminded him of them both. He thought it didn't show, but it was there in the slightest flicker of his eye, the smallest twitch of his brow.

Pain. Hurt. Loss.

So I did my best not to look like her. Phoebe was everything bold and bright and beautiful. She sang and she danced. She wore colourful dresses with plunging necklines and short hems. And without fail and despite the occasion, her lips always matched her nails. Her eyes flashed fun and mischief even though they were rimmed in darkness.

I hardly ever wore makeup. I dressed in jeans and t-shirts, sweaters and sneakers. I think it made it better. I didn't see that look in Dad's eye quite so often.

Half the pizza was gone and Dad's eyelids were drooping by the time I walked back into the lounge. The television channel had been changed. Coro was over and a quiz show was on. Dad sort of grunted himself awake when I sat on the couch, ankles tucked beneath my knees.

"Henry the eighth." Dad took a sip of whiskey, winking in my direction when the answer to his question proved correct. "Flatiron," he guessed for the next.

I dragged the blanket from the back of the couch over my lap then picked up my phone.

One missed call.

You.

10:53pm.

As I stared at the time, you called again. I left the room and shut my bedroom door. It wasn't that I didn't want Dad to know about you. It was that I wanted to know more about you before he did. Besides, what would I have said? That I gave my phone number to a stranger? That I met someone I was unexplainably drawn to? That I had spent the majority of my day thinking about you?

I swiped to accept. "Hi."

"Hi." There was a sigh on the other end of the line. I imagined you biting your lip. They were already a shade darker than what was deemed normal. Like they were bruised with passion.

"I know this will sound creepy-"

"Interesting way to start a conversation."

You laughed. Chuckled, really. "I'm an artist. Well, an art student." That explained the smudges of black and the sharpness to your scent.

"Congratulations?" I wasn't sure why you had called to tell

me this.

"I was wondering if you would allow me to draw you."

"Draw me?" I'd never been a huge conversationalist but it seemed around you, I was only capable of repeating the words you said.

"Yeah. I've debated all day about whether to call you, how best to broach the subject, but I couldn't come up with a way to ask without sounding creepy. So I decided just to own it. I…" There was an exhale of air again and I wondered if you were smoking. "I just can't get you out of my head. I figured maybe putting you on paper would help."

"You or me?" I asked.

"You or me what?"

"Who will it help?"

"Oh." Your voice fell. "Me. Just me. You can hang up if you like. I know this is strange. It's just, I'm in my first year of art school but I started off studying law. Got a couple of years under my belt before it dawned on me that I didn't want to be a lawyer. That was what the family wanted, you know?" You laughed again. "Sorry, I didn't mean to spill my life story. We can do something normal if you like. Go out for dinner? Get to know me a little before I start with the creepy stuff."

I don't know what it was about you that made my heart pound. Was it that you were a stranger? That I felt bold and daring talking to you? That I didn't feel like me?

I caught my reflection in the mirror and saw my sister.

"You can draw me."

"I can?"

Again, looking back now, I wonder what you thought in that moment. I made it so easy.

"When?" you asked.

"Now?" I regretted the word as soon as it came out of my mouth. "Unless that's too soon. Or too late. It's after eleven."

"It's perfect. Come on over. I'll order you a ride."

The voices inside my head screamed, telling me I was stupid to go to a stranger's house. It was dangerous. I didn't know anything about you. If I had, if I had known the truth, I would have never gone. But I was feeling brave and bold and foolish. I took off my slippers and pulled on my trainers. I discarded my t-shirt and instead chose to wear an oversized sweater, one that hung loosely off my frame and exposed the skin of one shoulder. I shrugged my jacket on and kissed my father goodnight. He was sleeping in the chair again. No doubt he would still be there when I got back. But just in case he woke, I scribbled a note on the pad stuck to the fridge.

Gone out. Home by two.

The car was waiting. The driver wasn't talkative, keeping his eyes on the road and the car filled with music so we didn't feel the need to converse. The air freshener stuck in the shutters of the heater gave me a headache as it mixed with the scent of cigarette smoke. It reminded me faintly of you. You smelled of smoke. Smoke and rain and paint.

I chewed on the nail of my index finger.

The driver still didn't say anything when we pulled up to your building. At first, I thought he must have made a mistake. It wasn't a house. It wasn't an apartment. It was an old shed in the industrial area. Bricks had fallen from the walls. One window was cracked. But the door opened and you were there, dressed in a white t-shirt and jeans, both covered in those dark smudges with the occasional splash of colour. Your feet were bare.

"You came."

I climbed out of the car. "I said I would."

"I wasn't sure." You stood back and opened the door. "Come in." Light crept out over the pavement. Heavy rock music slipped through the gap. I followed you inside.

"Sorry." You walked over to the stereo and turned it down. "I like music loud when I work."

I wasn't sure if I would have called what you were listening to music. It was more a mess of noise.

"Come over here. Take a look at some of my stuff."

It was warm inside. There was an open fire in one corner. I shrugged my jacket off and hung it on the back of a chair. There was nowhere else to put it. The shed was crammed full. Paint was splattered over the wooden panels of the floor, over chairs and walls. The sink was filled with discarded brushes and cans, and paint trailed as a rainbow of colour twisting to the plug hole. There was a mattress in one corner. It looked worn, slept in. A pizza box from my work was open on the table, though it was empty. The coffee machine on the bench had fingerprints of colour stained on the handle.

You flicked through a stack of canvases. "I prefer to work with charcoal." You pulled one out to show me. "Like this. This is how I want to draw you."

Instead of the colourful and brash paintings that covered the walls, the one you showed me was simple and understated. A mixture of harsh lines and smudges. Black and shades of grey.

"You're talented." And you were. There was something in your work, mostly in your portraits. It was like you could see the person behind them, the artist rather than the muse. The one you showed me of an old man sitting naked on a stool, arms crossed over his chest, his penis hidden by the cross of his legs, that one was my favourite. He must have looked straight at you as you did it. There was defiance in his stance. Like he didn't give a fuck. He looked like I wished I could be.

Walking over to the window, you placed a stool in front of it. "Here." You patted the stool. "Sit. Make yourself comfortable."

Like that was possible. You were too consuming.

I pulled myself onto the stool, lifting my shoulders high, my back straight. Adjusting myself, I tucked my feet behind the railing of the stool, then I took them off and let them fall, but it felt strange, like I was a child too small for the seat.

You were rummaging through shelves, discarding books and paint cans, stained coffee mugs and brushes, until you found a packet of cigarettes and shook it. There was one remaining so you took it out and held it between your lips.

"I don't know how you want me to sit."

I'm not sure if you knew what it felt like to have someone study you the way you studied me. I felt exposed under your gaze. I hadn't noticed it in the movie theatre but your eyes were a piercing blue. They turned my skin cold. Or maybe it was hot. I couldn't tell. With a box in your hands and an unlit cigarette in your mouth, you walked over to me, staring so intently I had to drop my gaze.

"Here." You lifted my chin with your finger. "Sit with your body to the window and look back over your shoulder." Your voice was muffled and the cigarette bounced up and down as you spoke.

I did as you instructed. Rain splattered across the window and blurred the lights of the city. I looked back at you over my shoulder. Your eyes fell over my body, assessing, contemplating. And then you stepped forward, sliding your hand around my neck, gathering my hair to let it fall down my back. You tugged on the sleeve of my sweater, exposing my shoulder.

Taking the cigarette out of your mouth, you said, "Perfect."

Walking over to the fire, you placed the cigarette between your lips and bent low, allowing the flame to lick the tip. I didn't know how you could stand so close and not shy away from the burn. Maybe you liked pain. "Are you okay to stay like that? Are you comfortable?"

I nodded and you pulled an easel from the wall, setting it up behind me. You were so close I could have reached out and touched you.

And then you started.

You chose each pencil carefully, but you didn't only use them. Your fingers became soiled in darkness as you smeared your work, sometimes rubbing furiously against the canvas and at other times using only the faintest of strokes. Most people painted with their hands but you used your entire body. Your mouth, full and red as it was, twisted and contorted with concentration even as the cigarette burned between your lips. Your feet shifted restlessly over the wooden floor.

I lost track of time as I sat there and watched you. Each time you looked up and found me staring, you locked your eyes on mine unabashedly. The ash of your cigarette fell to the floor. The tension was thicker than the smoke that filled the room. It compressed my chest, left me feeling naked and vulnerable.

"You know that's bad for you." I couldn't stand the silence any longer. I needed something, anything to break the tightness in my chest. Whatever it was.

You looked over at me and smiled. There was something so lazy about your expression. It could have been the way your eyelids drooped over your eyes. It could have been the slowness of your smile.

"Have you never done anything bad before, Sophie?"

"Not willingly, not something that I know would damage my health like smoking does."

You placed your pencil back in the box and took the cigarette out of your mouth, letting it fall to the floor and twisting it with the ball of your bare foot. You walked over, your silhouette outlined by the light of the streetlamp shining through the window, and stood before me.

"You've never wanted to do something bad? Never wanted to take control away from the people who say you can't?"

I thought about all the unanswered questions in my life and dropped my eyes. "Maybe."

I felt, rather than saw your hand reach out. You touched my cheek first. Just the faintest of strokes. Delicate. Soft. I lifted my gaze again and got trapped in yours. You were studying me. Your eyes skipped over my face, resting on each of my features, following the lines of my bones.

"Isn't the thrill of the experience more important than the result?"

Your hand slipped down my neck. I imagined the dark lines you left behind, tracing my body as though it were one of your paintings. Then your fingers wrapped around my throat. Not tight. But firm enough that you felt the rise and fall as I swallowed. Firm enough that it excited me.

It excited you too. Black flames licked your irises. Passion ignited your stance and you took a step closer. With your fingers digging into my flesh, you lowered your mouth to mine, searching for approval in my expression. Your lips were softer than I had imagined. But they burned. They scorched my skin, making it feel as though tiny layers peeled away under your touch. The pressure around my neck increased, tugging, pulling me to my feet as your kiss became more desperate. I pressed my body against yours and felt the firmness of you pressing back.

You were hard. I was soft.

I melted against you and a gasp or a moan escaped.

Releasing me, you tugged at the hem of your paint-stained t-shirt, pulling it over your head, revealing your nakedness. We stood looking at each other, chests rising and falling. Then your eyes trailed down my body and your hands reached out to take the hem of my sweater, slowly pulling it over my head until I too, stood bare before you.

My nipples hardened under your gaze, poking through the fabric of my bra. You looked up and then back down, a question floating across your features. I slid one strap down my shoulder. Then the other.

Your breathing quickened even more as I reached behind, unclasped the hook, and let the lace fall to the floor.

The appreciation in your eyes changed from an artist

inspecting his muse to that of a lover drinking in the curves of their beloved. Reaching out, you stroked a finger over the swell of my breast. Goosebumps prickled.

But with that touch, it was as though someone turned on the light in a darkened room and I could see again. I was blinded. Startled by the fact that I was there. With you. A stranger.

Stumbling back, I reached down to grab my discarded clothing, pulling it to my chest. "I should go."

Was it amusement or regret that splashed across your face? "I'm sorry." You reached out for me but stopped when I stepped away. "I moved too fast. I shouldn't have-"

"No. No. You didn't do anything I didn't want."

The sounds of the world had come back. Music played. Rain dropped on the tin roof. And then I saw the clock on the wall. Ten minutes past three. How had time eluded me so easily?

"Is that time right? I need to get home to my father."

You nodded, pulling your t-shirt back over your head, messing your hair and making me wish the lights in my brain had remained switched off.

I twisted, struggling with the hooks of my bra. "I told him I'd be home before two."

That's when you stepped closer. Your hands gently took hold of my arms and my skin prickled as you turned me and did up my bra. Your breath was hot as you whispered in my ear, "I didn't mean to scare you away."

My heart thumped. What was it about you that did this to me? Why did I feel as though my chest was about to explode? Why was it that I only felt this mixture of exquisite pain and pleasure when I was around you?

Your gaze was unsettling. "Will you come back to see my drawing once it's complete?"

I nodded. Or, at least I think I did. It was hard to know. I may have kissed you.

But when I walked out the door to the car waiting in the rain and I looked back over my shoulder, it was my sister's face I saw staring back at me from that canvas. I knew it wasn't mine because there was a beauty to it that could only ever belong to her.

three

I twisted my key in the lock quietly, not wanting to alert Dad to the fact that I was arriving home so late. He was still in his chair, light from the TV splashed across his face, empty whiskey bottle at his side.

There was a blanket I used for nights like this, and I placed it over Dad, folding it back under his chin and placing a kiss on his forehead. He stirred. He sighed and uttered the name of my sister.

I didn't turn the TV off, just turned down the volume. Somehow, I think it made it easier for him to sleep with noise in the background. Maybe they muted the voices of his own nightmares.

My bedroom was bigger than Dad's. It was the one he used to share with Mum, but after she died, he didn't want to sleep there anymore so it became Phoebe's and mine. We painted the walls, changed them from yellow to grey. I was only three when it happened. Phoebe was nine. Her pain was louder than mine. She remembered more. She remembered the knock of the police. The muttered words that told of the accident that killed her. I only remember my sister's tears.

Once Phoebe was gone, I kept the outline of the world map she had drawn on the only wall uninterrupted by windows or doors. She had painted it in one night as we talked about the places we wanted to see. She had a pile of old travel magazines and we cut out pictures of the Eiffel Tower, the pyramids of Giza, the Taj Mahal, the crystal clear beaches of Greece, anywhere and anything we wanted to see. We attached them to hooks of string and strung them over the drawing pins stuck on the map.

She often did things like that late at night. She would arrive home from a job, alive, awake and full of life and get me from my bed. She didn't like to be alone. Sometimes she would put on music and we would dance. Other times we would watch scary movies hiding under a blanket with only our eyes peeking out.

I ran my finger over the wall and watched the little pictures flutter with the disturbance. Flopping onto my bed, I pulled out my phone and checked the bank balance. Not too much more to go and then I could escape this place. I was almost free.

I must have fallen asleep like that as I woke a few hours later, fully dressed, someone pounding on the door.

Dad and I met in the kitchen, sharing a look of confusion over the table. Dad pulled the door open. Two policemen looked back at us.

"Are you Andrew Rush?"

Dad cleared his throat. "Can I help you?"

"It's about your daughter, Phoebe Rush. A body has been found and we think it's her."

four

My sister was a whore.

I first heard the word when I was twelve. I didn't know what it meant at the time, but Molly Ryan told me her uncle said that she was one. Phoebe just laughed when I told her. She never let things like that get to her. She sat me down and held onto my shoulders, looking straight into my eyes. "A whore is what people call women when they are threatened by them. It says more about the person who uses it than the person it is used to describe."

I already knew it wasn't a nice word. I could tell by the way Molly said it. She almost spat it. She was probably just copying her uncle. As I grew older I knew why people used it. I knew it was because of her job. People didn't see that my sister provided for us in ways my father never could. They didn't see that she was happy. That she was free. That she chose that life.

They only saw a whore.

When she first went missing the headlines in the local

paper and the news referred to her as a prostitute. Missing Prostitute Phoebe Rush. Some called her an escort. Some an exotic dancer. One even called her a lady of the night. As though it were the darkness that was the issue.

My sister always held her head high. She always smiled. She would smile while attending school meetings or assemblies where people would talk behind her back and quietly refuse her assistance in place of my absent parents. She would laugh and tell me that it was her secret weapon for getting out of it.

She was strong. I never once saw her hang her head. I never once saw her bend to their vicious words. The only time she ever apologised for her chosen profession was when it affected me. If she could have shielded me, she would have. But she told me that people chose to be cruel. She told me that was their choice and I didn't have to be the same.

There was only ever one person she lied to about her job. She told our father she was an assistant to an important businessman. And she was. Sort of. She assisted many men, just not in the way our father imagined.

Her clients were professionals. Her dates required glamourous dresses, dramatic makeup and real jewels. I tried to sell some of it after she disappeared, the money would have helped. But each time I managed to sneak a few pieces to the pawn shop, Dad always found out and spent more money getting them back. He couldn't stand for anyone else to have a piece of her. Now, all her belongings were locked away as a shrine to her memory.

She was careful. Safe. Protected.

Until that night.

She said goodbye like she always said goodbye. With a kiss and a smile. It wasn't a new job. It was a place she had been before. She knew the men. She knew the parties. She knew what was expected of her. Nothing other than to socialise and laugh and dance. As normal, nothing else was required and any further arrangements made were strictly hers to approve.

Benedict Walsh was the last man to see her. He said she danced, she laughed and chatted with some of the guests. She had a drink. Maybe two. And then she got into a taxi and left.

But he couldn't remember the name of the taxi company.

It was too dark to see the colour of the car.

And every taxi company contacted by the police had no record of collecting her from that address.

She simply disappeared.

Dad and I were left in limbo, not knowing what happened. We no longer knew how to live. We couldn't smile without feeling guilty. We couldn't laugh without wondering if she was out there somewhere, unable to laugh herself. Maybe she was held captive. Maybe she was hurt, injured, waiting for someone to find her.

My father walked the roads around the Walsh's residence.

He always suspected them. But they were wealthy. They were well respected. They helped the police. And despite his insistence that Benedict Walsh was behind her disappearance, he was never believed. He was the father of a whore.

After a while, I accepted that there was only one reason for her not to walk through our door. She was dead. And while I gave up hope, my father drank to forget.

five

"Are you okay?"

My father was back in his chair. We had spent the day at the police station, listening to their explanation. Feeling nothing.

Dad stared at the TV. The news had already hit. Local Prostitute Phoebe Rush's body found in the trunk of a car at the bottom of the lake. They showed her photo again. The same one that always accompanied her story. It wasn't one that showed her smile, the naturalness of her beauty. It was one from her business profile. Sultry. Seductive. One that fitted into their narrative.

Dad hadn't said much as we sat in the small office with grey walls and slats across the windows. The policeman explained that a jogger had recently gone missing while on the running tracks around the estuary. He went for a run and never came back. It turned out later that he had skipped town. Wanted to start a new life with a new wife and a new family. But before they discovered that, they sent divers into the water to search for his body. Instead, they found a car. One that had been reported missing years ago. A year before my sister went missing.

A year before she was killed.

They dragged the car to the surface. They popped the trunk. They found my sister.

Do you know what a body looks like after four years under water? Neither do I, because they wouldn't let us see. But they knew it was her because the DNA told them so.

Nothing had changed, except now we knew. She was dead. She would never walk through that door with a smile on her face and an outlandish story of where she had been. She would never hold my hands and dance in the light shining through the window. She would never add another picture to our map.

The news was rehashing old details. It showed Walsh and his clueless wife standing solemnly at the memorial service held a year after she went missing. Dad hadn't wanted them there. Neither had I. Their presence was a slap in our faces. A knife dug into our hearts.

The police had re-opened the case, not that it was ever officially closed. They had reached a dead end. They had given up. Now they were pleading with the public again. They were calling for witnesses of the car, of any strange happenings at the old boatshed that sat on the edge of the estuary.

They released the new information that her hands and feet were bound. They were going to look into her clients. Again.

I looked over at Dad and repeated the question. "Are you

okay?"

He didn't answer. Instead, he smiled a sad smile and reached for the bottle. He wasn't always this way. He was just lost without her. Mum dying had beaten him down. Phoebe's disappearance had shattered what was left.

My phone rang and I grabbed it quickly. The ringtone was too bright. Too cheerful.

It was Jess. "Why didn't you call me?"

"I-"

She didn't let me finish. "I'm coming over. This requires alcohol. Lots of alcohol."

Later, we sat in my bedroom, staring at the map on the wall, hiding from the unshed tears in my father's eyes.

"We should go out. You need to dance. You need to drink and dance and forget."

I laughed, feeling strangely cold, empty. I thought finding her body would bring a sense of closure. But all it did was create more questions. "What would people think?"

"Fuck people." Jess tipped a bottle of beer to her mouth.

"I really don't think that will help."

Dad knocked on the door and opened it a crack. He nodded to Jess. "I can't be here. I'm heading to the pub."

"Do you think that's a good idea?" The pub was Dad's second home. The place he went when the silence got too loud.

"No. Probably not. But I'm going anyway. What are you girls up to for the night?"

"I'm trying to convince her we should hit the club." Jess grinned softly at Dad as though smiling too widely might break him.

"Good idea."

I looked over at him, surprised. "It's a terrible idea."

"Sometimes terrible ideas are the best ideas. You should go. It would do you good to have some fun."

"I don't feel like having fun." And then the pain hit. Those were words I could remember saying to my sister when she would drag me out of bed in the wee hours of the morning. I was tired. I had school the next day. I didn't feel like having fun. I wanted to sleep. But she would never listen. She would pull the blankets off the bed, turn up the music and start dancing until eventually she would win me over and we would sing at the top of our lungs. Our neighbours sometimes complained. But Dad never did.

I sighed. "Fine. I'll go."

six

I don't know how long we were at the nightclub before I noticed you, because when I looked up, your eyes were already on me. You didn't smile. You didn't nod your head in recognition. You just stared, leaning against the bar, elbows propped on the counter.

Music pumped like blood through my veins. Coloured lights illuminated your face in flashes. Red. Blue. Green. Yellow. You held a glass in your right hand and occasionally brought it to your lips, a sip at a time. Surrounding you were all the same people from the movie theatre. At least I thought they were. They looked the same. Dressed the same. But you weren't paying attention to any of them.

Even though I looked like my sister, the only time I felt like her was when I danced.

I was free.

I was alive.

Music moved my body in ways nothing else could. Nothing else ever would. Except you.

You watched but you never moved. You didn't come over

to talk to me. You didn't jerk your head, inviting me to join you. But it wasn't until one of your friends bumped into you that you turned away from me and back to them.

Just like I did in the movie theatre, I felt the loss of you. And even though you didn't owe me a thing, not a word, a glance, or a kiss, disappointment replaced the music in my veins. The people previously made invisible by the pulse of the bass jostled against my body. Sweat covered my skin. My eyes burned with the fog that was shot from machines and swirled around my feet.

I needed to breathe.

Stumbling my way through the crowd, I headed for the back door, drawing in a gasp of fresh air as soon as I made it outside. People were smoking and they looked at me curiously. Leaning against the concrete wall, the cool breeze of the night danced over my skin, prickling it with goosebumps.

"You should come and see the finished product."

Heat flooded through me just at the sound of your voice. I was back there. At your place. Naked and exposed. Bared for you.

Pulling myself from the wall, I willed myself to appear calm, unflustered. But I don't think it worked because you smiled at me in a way that said you knew my innermost thoughts.

"Now?"

You tilted your head so the tip of your cigarette met the

flame between your fingers. "Do you want to keep dancing?"

"I'm with Jess."

"The bouncy one? She can come too."

I laughed. Jess did bounce when she danced, but only when she was drunk. But I didn't want Jess to know what I had done. I didn't want her to know that you drew the lines of my body.

I didn't want to share.

But as if uttering her name was magic, the door swung open and she appeared.

"There you are!" She rolled her eyes as though it was something I often did, running away. Then she saw you. "You again." Her eyes narrowed. "Are you stalking us now?"

"Yes." You said it so openly that no one would have ever suspected it to be true.

I looped my arm through hers, feeling how hot and sweaty her skin was in comparison to mine which was now cold to the touch. "Killian's an artist. He invited us back to his place to see some of his stuff."

Jess rolled her eyes. "Because that doesn't sound creepy." She walked over and took the cigarette from between your lips, bringing it to her own and sucking in the poisonous air. "You may as well be wearing a t-shirt with a lollipop on the front saying 'suck me'."

"It's okay. I've been there before." The words were out before I realised I had revealed my secret.

Jess turned on her heels slowly, pulling the cigarette out of her mouth and letting the puff of smoke into the night. "Don't tell me. He invited you back to his place and asked you to 'model' for him." She gave you back the cigarette but you threw it to the ground and crushed it under your shoe. "OMG, he did. Sophie, what is wrong with you? He could have been a serial killer!"

"I'm still here, aren't I?"

You didn't say anything during this exchange. You stood there watching, your eyes showing disdain for the world, your skin pale under the glow of the streetlamp and your mouth bruised and kissable.

Jess tugged on my arm and dragged me away, not far enough that you couldn't hear what we were saying though. You looked on with interest, pulling another cigarette from the packet and placing it between your lips.

I had never been jealous of an inanimate object before.

"What's going on?" Jess hissed. "Why didn't you tell me you'd seen this guy again?"

I shrugged. "It was nothing. He's an art student."

"He doesn't look like a fucking art student to me."

The door opened again and one of your friends poked his head out. "You coming back in?"

You looked up and shook your head, letting smoke escape as a vapour out your nostrils. It was disgustingly sexy. I wanted you to treat me with the same filthy adoration.

"I like him, Jess." It was best to tell her the truth. There was no way she would have let me leave with you otherwise, and in that moment there was nothing I wanted more.

For you to grip me in your arms.

To have your mouth on my flesh.

To be used by you.

"Fine." Jess huffed. "But you text me his address as soon as you get there. And his full name. And his phone number." Letting go of me she walked towards the door that led back into the club. "And a photo of him or possibly a copy of his driver's license." She gave you the signal that she was watching you, fingers pointed at her eyes then at yours, and disappeared back into the chaos.

You were blowing smoke rings into the air. Anyone else, and I would have turned away from such a flagrant display. But not you. With you, I was transfixed.

"So you're coming home with me?"

It sounded so dirty coming from your mouth, as though I had agreed to more than just seeing your finished artwork. I wondered if you could see it in my eyes. The lust. The longing.

Swallowing the nervous knot at the back of my throat, I nodded.

And your eyes got stuck on the flesh of my neck.

seven

I was naked on your canvas.

Earlier, when I had left in a rush, it was only the lines of my sister's face that looked back at me. Now, she was gone and I was there. It was my face staring back at me through wide and innocent eyes. My hair that flowed down my naked back. The cheeks of my backside that rested full and round on the stool. Despite you never seeing my full nakedness, you had drawn me perfectly.

You leaned against the wall and pulled a knife from your pocket, rolling it between your fingers in an endless display of confident defiance. My eyes were drawn to you as much as they were to the painting. You were so casual, so cocky.

"Do you like it?" You placed the knife back in your pocket and moved to stand behind me. I could feel the heat of you. Your mouth was close to my ear. The scent of stale smoke drowned my senses.

"You're good."

Your smile was slow and drawn out as it crept across your mouth. It was everything arrogant, seductive and true. "I know."

I moved closer to the portrait and further from you. "I'm naked."

You stepped around me so your fingers could brush over the canvas. "You're beautiful."

I almost believed you.

"Come." You held out your hand and I took it. "I'm sure I've got something to drink here somewhere." Depositing me on an overstuffed couch next to the fire, you rustled through the contents of the shelving. I took the chance to look around the room once again. It was just as messy as before. Your bed—which was just a mattress on the floor—was dishevelled. Sheets hung over the edge and were strewn across the floor. The pizza box was gone, thrown into the large bin serving as trash collection in the corner and in its place were empty kebab wrappers.

After a few minutes of searching, you found a bottle of vodka and held it up as a question. I nodded. You gave up on finding a glass and took a swig straight from the mouth. I did the same, shuddering as the warmth of it hit the back of my throat.

You looked at me curiously. "What's the matter?"

I coughed a little, clearing the burn. "What makes you think something is the matter?"

"I could tell by the way you danced. You were dancing to forget." You took another gulp of the vodka. "Or maybe you were dancing to remember."

I wondered how you knew this about me. Of course, I didn't know what you knew. I was innocent. Naïve. Too easily swept up by you. It should have been plain that you had watched me before.

I shifted closer to the flames. Closer to you. "My sister." I didn't say anything more as there was a tightness in my chest restricting my words.

You had to prompt me. "Is she okay?"

I shook my head, trying to will away the swell of tears that threatened to spill. "She's dead." And then they fell.

You took me in your arms. Rocking me. Stroking my hair as I cried. I don't know why I cried with you when I didn't earlier. Not when the police told me they knew it was her. Not when they explained that her feet and hands were bound. Not even when my father bowed his head and his shoulders shook. Then, I had to be brave. I had to be strong. But around you I felt safe. I could crumble.

"When?" You looked at me with such concern, such tenderness, there was no way I could have known the truth.

"She went missing three years ago. The police have just discovered her body."

Knowledge lit your expression. "The prosti-" You stopped yourself when you saw the pain flick across my eyes. "I saw it on the news." You sat back on the couch, your arm casually slung over the back, one foot resting on the knee of the other. "Tell me about her." You must have sensed the panic that hit my chest because you added, "If you want."

There was something in your eyes. In the way you looked at me.

I poured my heart out and in the process I lost it to you.

I told you of the ridicule she faced. Of the cruel words and the ugly hearts of the people that never understood her. I told you how we danced. How we dreamed. I told you of the desperation and loss my father now carried like a blanket.

I told you everything.

And that was when I started to imagine my life with you. Our children with your eyes and my hair. The studio where you would paint. The cover of my memoir which told of our trip around the world that served as your inspiration and my salvation.

You never stopped watching me as I exposed my soul. I couldn't meet your eye. There was too much said in your expression.

"I lost someone too." I heard the pain in your voice. Recognised it. "She just slipped away in my hands." You looked down at your hands resting on your lap as though they were responsible for your loss. "I think I could have loved her. We could have been good together. But maybe now I've got a second chance."

You were gentle at first. Just a hand on my knee. But even that innocent touch left me burnt.

I ached for you.

Craved you.

I wanted to be consumed by you.

So I inched closer and lifted my head. I saw myself reflected in your eyes. I saw desperation, adoration and desire.

Leaning further, I held my breath until my lips brushed against yours. And then your hands were in my hair. And your mouth devoured mine with all the pent-up lust I had seen lingering in your eyes. My fingers fumbled with the buttons of your shirt.

I had to see you.

All of you.

We were a feverish rush of entwined limbs and discarded clothing, lustful mouths and quivering hands. I found myself on the mattress beneath you as your mouth sucked in my nipple.

I hissed or sighed or gasped.

"I need to see you." The words came out as pants, such was my desire to study the landscape of your body.

You slowed down, drawing away from me with hooded eyes and lips so red they looked as though they were stained with blood. You got to your feet. I got to mine. We stood opposite each other and you allowed me to study you. You didn't look away. You never tried to hide. And that gave me the boldness I needed.

I traced the swells of your chest. You were smooth and slender. I could see the lines of your ribs as well as the ripples of your stomach.

You were beautiful.

Your cock stood tall and proud. Unashamed under my scrutiny. It was as though your body knew I adored it.

Reaching between us, you took my hand and placed it on your chest. The steady thud of your heart echoed. Controlling my hand with your own, you ran it over the dips and swells of your flesh, across your chest, your shoulders, the flat plane of your stomach, and the nest of dark hair, then finally, your hardness. I wondered if you saw the need in my eyes as you wrapped my fingers around your erection and guided me to stroke you. I wondered if you noticed the flex of my thighs, the sharpness of my breath as it caught in my chest.

You left me there, wrapped around you as your hand cupped my face. I pushed against it, relishing the contrasting feel of your hardness in one hand and the softness of my skin under your fingers. Threading your fingers through my hair, you pulled my head back, exposing my neck. Leaning forward, you ran your tongue from the dip of my collarbones to the curve of my jaw. Wide and soft. Like velvet. My hand tightened on your cock. You increased the grip on my hair. It tugged against my scalp as pain. But pain I wanted. Pain I needed. Your grip had a paralysing effect, freezing my body in an arc towards you, breasts straining and demanding attention. I wanted to climb inside, feel your body devour mine.

Moving your lips down my body, you took one nipple between your teeth, making me cry out. You grew harder in my hand and thrust against me with a grunt.

And then I was on the floor. The wood was rough under my shoulder blades, but you twisted me over, holding my arms out wide and crushing my breasts. Not one inch of me was left untouched by your tongue and your hands. Your cock dragged over my skin, leaving soft trails of precum in its wake.

I was drugged with desire. The world evaporated and there was nothing left but me and you.

I wasn't sure if it was the vodka, the stress of the day, or simply you, but slivers of time vanished. I was pressed to the hard wooden floor. I was spread across the table with your mouth hovering over the apex of my thighs, teasing and taunting me until I wanted to take fistfuls of your hair and force your mouth onto me. My back was slammed against a wall, your arm hooked under my thigh and your cock rubbing me, sliding over my entrance with the moisture of my desire.

And then we were on the mattress again and you rose over me, nestling between my thighs, forcing them apart with the pressure of your hands. Exposed. Vulnerable. Eager.

You played with yourself as you watched me. Your eyes were fixated on my nakedness. With one hand you stroked yourself and with the other you stroked me. I writhed under your attention.

I begged for you.

You gave me what I wanted. What I asked for. You

pushed inside. And I stretched for you, my lip caught between my teeth, trapped in this moment of exquisite rapture.

If someone had told me then what you did, what you would do, I would have cursed their name. I would have ripped their tongue from their mouth.

For in that moment, I would have died for you.

I would have killed for you.

Burned for you.

That was how you made me feel.

Like you were worth something.

Worth everything.

You fucked me hard. Your thrusts were sharp and deep. Each time you moved within me, I moaned and gasped. Grabbing my hips, you jerked me closer. Then your hands travelled up my body, crushing my breasts, pinching my nipples until my toes curled, my head thrashing against the mattress.

And then your hand slipped around my neck. Just one. No pressure. No threat to my airway, but the thought of it excited me. You held me in place and thrust in and out. And then your fingers pulsed, tightening just enough to make me squirm.

Euphoria rippled. You saw it in my eyes and lifted another hand to my neck, increasing the pressure. Your eyes bore into mine as you continued to fuck with your hands wrapped around my neck. I found it hard to breathe but the effect it had on me was not one of panic or fear. It was one of desire and lust. My orgasm came so quickly, it caught me by surprise. My body was on fire. Release licked my skin and exploded within me in a way I had never felt before. Because of you.

You fucked me harder. You pushed me further. I felt lightheaded and far away, but my body was grounded by the thrust of your cock and the pressure of your hands. Then your fingers tightened more and I couldn't breathe. Panic crashed like a wave and it excited you. I saw it in your eyes. I felt it in the way you turned to steel.

Gripping onto your forearms, I strained against you, pushing you away, shaking my head with what little movement you allowed me.

But you were stronger.

You were lost with desire.

You were gone.

"Please," I gasped through vocal cords stretched too far. Letting go of your arms, I dug my nails into your chest, drawing them down and leaving bloody and jagged lines behind.

Your hands flew away. Fear and regret focused your eyes and your body fell towards mine, scooping my head in your hands and pulling me to your chest.

"I'm sorry. I'm so so sorry." You still thrust inside me but now you were gentle and I was frozen. Stroking my hair you whispered in my ear, pleading with me to forgive you. "I'm sorry. I didn't mean to scare you. I got carried away. I'm so sorry. Please forgive me."

Our sweat-covered bodies pressed against each other. Your chest slid over mine with each rock of your hips. Your lips moved against my ear, my face, my mouth and my neck as you mumbled apologies.

I lay limp beneath you as you peppered kisses of regret across my flesh. There were wooden beams that crisscrossed over the ceiling. Splatters of red paint had reached some of them and I wondered how they got there. The flames of the fire had died to embers. The bottle of vodka was on the floor beside your mattress, liquid oozing onto the wood.

You thrust once more. Hard. And then you came.

"Are you okay?" You lifted your head lazily to look at me. A smile played with the corners of your blood-red lips.

I shook my head. Or maybe I nodded. I think I smiled.

"That was amazing." You rolled off me, your hand falling to your forehead as you gazed up at the wooden beams of the ceiling. "Sorry I got carried away. But you liked it, didn't you? Before, I mean. Before I took it too far."

I shook my head. Or maybe I nodded. I think I smiled.

"I knew you would," you said. "I knew it the moment I saw you. You and I are the same. We have a connection." You rolled onto your side, propping your head up with your hand. I flinched when you reached out to brush your finger over my neck, but I didn't move away. I didn't tell you to stop.

"They are so beautiful."

I wondered what you were talking about. You didn't say I was so beautiful. You said they.

I sat up, scared by the way my body trembled. "I need to use the bathroom."

You were fumbling through the pockets of your jeans on the floor. "Right over there." And you nodded to a door, grinning triumphantly when you found your packet of cigarettes and shook it so one popped out.

The mirror in your bathroom was mottled and green around the edges. My naked reflection stared back and I saw what 'they' were.

Bruises. They matched the ridges of your fingers. I had never been marked by someone before. Never been bruised by someone's touch. I had seen them on my sister, even though she tried to hide them. It had only happened once, that I knew of, and I only knew because I saw her through the crack of the bathroom door. She was crying and feathering her fingers over her skin reverently. Then the door shut.

I closed my eyes and was taken back to when I came with your hands around me. Was this what I wanted? Was this what I asked for? Had my body betrayed me by responding in such a way?

I swallowed and it hurt.

After using the toilet, I walked back to you. You were still lying on the mattress, cigarette between your teeth, naked body spread over the sheets, your cock flaccid and content between your thighs.

I bent to pick up my dress, but your fingers wrapped around my wrist. "Don't go," you pleaded. "Stay with me."

I shook my head. Or maybe I nodded. I think I smiled.

And I climbed back on the mattress beside you. With your arm around my shoulder, you pulled me close. I watched as tendrils of smoke escaped your mouth and floated to the rafters.

"Thank you." You stretched away from me to press the stub of your cigarette into the floor. "Thank you for staying."

And then you fell asleep.

I didn't think I would fall asleep but I did. With my head pressed against your chest, somehow, I still felt safe in your arms.

eight

I woke with your mouth against my bruises, your tongue lapping as though you could taste them.

Did they taste of fear?

Did they taste of pleasure?

Did they taste of obsession?

My body had already begun to respond despite my lack of consciousness and I was wet. Even in sleep my body desired you. You moved over me, kissing and licking. Your hand slid between us and you moaned when you found me so ready. You kissed me and I kissed you. And then you were inside me again and my body throbbed as though it had missed you. As though it had felt the loss of you.

My mind went back to the night before, the way your fingers wrapped around my neck, the light-headedness of my desire. A wave of humiliation swept over me but rather than dissipating, it rolled into desire, starting in the pit of my stomach and spreading until every inch of me throbbed. I dug my fingers into your back and you hissed.

You liked pain.

You tore my hands away and held them above my head, pressing them into the pillow, my wrists trapped. Then you bit my shoulder. Your teeth sank into my flesh and I cried out.

The lazy haze of sleep had left your eyes and you reached one hand between our bodies to roughly twist my nipple. I cried out again but my body arched towards you, begging for more. Letting go of my wrists, you pressed your hand over my mouth and twisted my nipple harder.

I bit you.

It felt so wrong.

So filthy.

So desperate.

You slapped me.

I came.

It was a shuddering orgasm that rippled through me violently and unexpectedly. You came too, and we lay threaded together in a mixture of heavy breathing, sweat and shame.

I didn't know if this was how you usually fucked. I didn't know if this was your thing, but you acted as though it were. You lifted yourself off me and grinned, reaching once again for that post-coital poison. You lit it then rubbed my arm either in appreciation or dismissal. I wasn't sure which because I had never done anything like that before. I had never experienced something that I was both ashamed and aroused by.

"You want to come to my exhibit tonight?" You looked at me, your eyes roaming over my body, lingering on the bruises that ringed my neck. "My family is out of town and I'd love someone there." You blew smoke into the air. "Only if you want to." Lifting yourself off the bed, you walked to the bathroom. The stream of your piss hitting the toilet bowl crept through the open door. Gathering my clothes from the floor, I pulled my dress on, not bothering with underwear.

You came back out, leaned against the wall, cigarette in your mouth, one eye slightly closed to protect it against the smoke, one eyebrow cocked and waiting for my answer.

"What time?" I asked as I tugged my shoes on. They gripped my feet painfully.

"Seven. I have to be there early, but I could send a car to collect you."

I shrugged my shoulders. "Sure. Sounds good."

"It will have artwork from everyone in my class. It's a group exhibition. You want a coffee?"

The machine on the bench was black and chrome. Despite the fingerprints of paint, it looked nothing like what a struggling artist could afford.

"I better go. Dad will worry. I never told him I wasn't coming home last night." Picking up my phone, I checked for missed calls from my father. There were none, but there were three from Jess. Plus numerous text messages threatening that if I turned up dead the next day she would never forgive me.

You smirked. "You're twenty-one years old and still have to ask for permission to stay out the night?"

It was another clue I missed.

"He just worries, you know? With Mum and Phoebe and all."

Your smile dropped. "Sorry. That was thoughtless of me."

"It's okay."

"You didn't tell me about your mum."

I swallowed and it hurt. "She died too," was all I said.

I didn't know how to say goodbye. Did I kiss you? Hug you? Slap you? But you took the dilemma away when you walked over and placed a chaste kiss on my nose. Well, I thought it was chaste, but your cock still twitched with arousal.

"See you tonight?" You said it as a question, your mouth still pressed against my nose. Then you walked away without my answer, grabbing a scarf from a hook on the wall. "Here, you might need this."

I nodded.

I smiled.

I wrapped the scarf around my neck and I left.

nine

"Where have you been?" Dad looked at me angrily but I knew that it was just fear.

"I'm sorry I didn't call." I pressed a kiss to the top of his head and wondered if I smelled of you. "It was easier just to spend the night with Jess."

Dad didn't smile. "That would have been why she called looking for you then." He narrowed his eyes in a knowing way but didn't press further. There were things fathers didn't want to know about their daughters.

"It's all over the news." Dad turned his attention back to the television. "She's everywhere."

Sure enough, the sultry image of my sister stared back at me. I couldn't help but think of her in the back of that car, trapped in the boot. Was she alive when it plunged into the water? Did she wait in desperation for someone to rescue her then finally succumb, gulping in water when her lungs could take no more?

I shook my head, trying to clear away the mental images and adjusted the scarf around my neck.

ten

I wore a black dress. One with no sleeves and a high neck. You had to be there early, so I arrived alone. You spotted me as soon as I walked through the door and wove your way through the crowd to greet me. You pressed a kiss to my cheek, cupping my face with your hand, your little finger slipping under the neck of my dress and stroking the tender flesh.

"You came." You said it as though you were surprised, as though you had expected me to run away and never want to see you again.

I should have.

"Come over and take a look at my work. You haven't seen these ones before."

And there I was, on display for the world to see. My eyes. My face. My neck. Three paintings in a row. Colourful and messy.

"When did you do these?" The paint was thick and raised from the canvas. My skin was red and blue, green and yellow. My hair was a rainbow.

You laughed. It was the first and only time I heard you laugh like that. Loud. Unabashed. I thought it was the real you. "Do you like them?"

I could say without a hint of dishonesty they were the best on display. Your work was amazing, your talent undeniable. Everyone in the room knew it. Your fellow students looked on with envy and your teacher with pride. She kept pulling you away from me to hear the praises of potential clients.

I wondered what you saw in me, what made you choose me as your muse when there were so many other women who adored you.

I was no one. Nothing. Just a girl who worked at a pizza shop and was saving what little money she earned so she could leave the only place she'd ever called home.

You were someone. Everything. A boy who dripped with talent, who had the world at their feet, who deserved more than a girl like me.

"So you're Ronan's latest muse?" The voice was cold and low. I turned to find dark eyes fixed on me, mockery posed in her expression.

"Ronan?" I looked over to your painting. My eyes focused on the scribble of a signature in the corner. Ronan Killian.

This girl, this woman who clearly had feelings for you, stepped closer and tugged at the collar of my dress. I jerked away.

She smiled coldly. "I see he hasn't changed."

There was a straw in the drink she held and she chased it

around the glass with her lips. "I was his muse once. Before his tastes changed and he preferred his victims to come from the other side of the tracks." Her eyes moved up and down my body, unimpressed. I recalled seeing them painted in black on one of the canvases in your shed.

"Lenora." Your voice was cold when you said her name. "What are you doing here?"

She swatted your arm playfully, eyes gleaming. "To see you, silly. Your parents told me about this little exhibit so I thought I'd pop along to support you." She pouted, glossy and plump lips ringed in pink. "I thought you'd be pleased." Chasing the straw around the glass again, she grinned when she caught it and lowered her lips, looking over the rim of her glass before pulling up in slow seduction.

Your body grew tense. "You can leave now."

She smiled and bit down on the straw. Hard. Something flickered in your eyes. Lust. Repulsion. I wasn't sure.

"Don't be like that," she cooed. Then she smiled. "It was nice to meet you…" She paused and shrugged. "Whoever you are." And then she sauntered off, swaying her hips as though she knew, or hoped you were watching. But you weren't. I turned to find your eyes burning.

"I'm sorry. I didn't know she would be here."

I started to reply, to tell you there was no need to apologise, but I caught a flash of a couple across the room and my heart leapt in panic. My blood turned cold and I tugged on your arm. "I need to leave."

You followed the line of my vision. You saw the panic in my eyes and pulled me away.

"Is that them?" you asked. I had told you of them the night before. How my father was certain they played a role in my sister's death. How they turned up at her service, not in support of our loss, but as a statement of their innocence.

They dripped in wealth and privilege. Her hair was blunt and cold and blonde. Her neck was encased in gold. His hair was thick and full and dark. His suit was tailored and tapered to perfection. They were looking my way with pained expressions. My breath caught in my throat. My heart raced. Part of me wanted to storm over to them, demand an explanation. She wasn't missing anymore. She was dead. They had to know something. He was the last person to see her alive. I wanted to know if she really believed his claim. If she was certain he had no part in her death.

But you took my hand, ignoring the call of your name from your instructor and ushered me outside. The cold air was a welcome relief. It allowed me to breathe again. But when I looked over my shoulder and through the glass of the window, I could make out their frames, weaving through the crowd, heading my way, and once again my breath became heavy and stuck in my chest.

I turned to you. "Take me away."

Hand in hand, we started to run. There was something exhilarating about running down that street with you. The wind rushing by us, our hands gripped together, cars speeding by in the blur. Excitement rose in my chest, but I couldn't say why. Laughter threatened to bubble as I reached down and tugged my shoes from my feet.

"Come on," you urged, even though they were far in the distance, staring down the road at us in confusion. "Keep going."

I thought it was because you wanted to protect me. Because you wanted to shield me from them, from their past, from my past so I ran with you, blissfully unaware. Blissfully ignorant in my giddiness.

When our steps slowed and we panted with exertion, you hailed a taxi and we climbed in. Your phone buzzed. The screen told me it was your mother but you powered it off, too busy laughing with me. Too busy sucking in the air that our lungs craved.

"That was close." You took my hand and ran your thumb over the flesh. "You okay?"

"I wonder what they were doing there?"

You shrugged. "Maybe they knew one of the students. Most of them are merely rich kids who consider themselves creative."

It seemed like a reasonable explanation. And it was. Because it was the truth.

You unlocked the door to your shed with a large key. The lock groaned, then the door groaned when you pushed it open. The room had not changed from the last time I was here, but it felt different. This time it felt familiar. Safe. It felt like home.

Tossing my shoes into the corner, you caught me from behind, wrapping your arms around my waist, my back to your chest, and twirled me about the room. My laughter filled the space.

Then you put me down and I turned in your arms. We were face to face. Inhaling each other's breath. And then your lips were on mine in a feverish passion. Your hands were on my body and mine were on yours. I fumbled with the buttons of your shirt, and once released, I tossed it away. You reached for the hem of my dress, your fingers caressing my thighs and my side as you lifted the material up and over my head. Your mouth dove to my neck and I stretched back for you, open and vulnerable. But then you pulled back, eyes dancing.

"I want to paint you." Your voice came out in a rush. "I want you to pose for me. Would you do that? Would you pose for me?"

At first I was a little confused. I had already posed for you. You had already recorded the lines of my face. But then it dawned on me when your eyes fell to my body, what you meant.

"Please?" You sensed my hesitation. All the confidence and exhilaration had fled my stance.

Without waiting for my reply, you slipped one of the straps of my bra over my shoulder. Then the other. Each touch licked my flesh with fire. Walking behind me, you undid the hooks of my bra and it fluttered to the floor. Your hands stroked my legs as you removed my underwear. And then I was naked before you.

Nervousness descended. I stood, one hand clutching the wrist of the other across my belly, one knee bent and floating out to the side, the ball of that foot twisting into the wooden panels of the floor.

"I don't know how to stand."

You had already pulled your easel into the centre of the room. A palette was in your hand. "Just like that. Stay exactly as you are."

Your brush moved furiously over the canvas. My world closed in and nothing else existed. There was only you and me and the strokes of your brush.

And then the door creaked open and they walked in. I was confused. It should have been obvious then, but I couldn't put the pieces together. I scrambled for the sheet off the mattress to cover myself as Mrs Walsh walked over, a look of disgust on her face, and muttered, "Oh, dear god."

Benedict Walsh looked at me greedily. His eyes travelled over me as though he could see through the fabric of the sheet, as though he knew what was underneath. Then he winked at you.

"What are you doing here?" I was still shocked with confusion.

Brianna Walsh looked over at me in surprise. "I'm sorry, but do I know you?" She had no idea who I was. They had no idea who I was. It was plain in the way they stared at me. There was no recognition, no remorse or embarrassment. To them I was no one. Nothing. It should have clicked for me then but it didn't.

I was too busy adoring you to be suspicious of you.

"What are you doing here?" you echoed my question.

"We flew all the way back from London, just to see your little exhibition, and you literally ran away from us." Brianna Walsh looked around the room for the first time. She was not impressed. "Ronan, please tell me you haven't been sleeping here. It's so filthy. You'll come home tonight, won't you?"

It was only then that it hit me. You weren't just Killian. You weren't even Ronan Killian. You were Ronan Killian Walsh, son of Benedict and Brianna Walsh.

My world crashed. The sensations of the city closed in, overwhelming me as they slipped through the open door. Motor oil. Pavement wet with rain. The faint aroma of freshly baked bread.

The overhead light spluttered on and off as though it too shared my surprise. My thoughts were sluggish. I had the pieces. I just couldn't put them together.

I needed to escape. Gathering my dress from the floor and my shoes from the corner, I clutched them in my hand, the sheet still twisted around me and dragging behind like a veil.

I met your eyes, those beautiful, piercing blue eyes. "It's not what you think," you said.

There was such desperation in your expression, such pleading. I looked over at your parents and was met with confusion.

"Ronan, tell me what is going on this instant." Benedict Walsh's voice was a command.

I didn't wait to hear your answer. With my shoes and dress stuffed between my fingers, I ran out the door, tears welling and your gaze burning into my back.

"It's not what you think," you yelled out again.

But that was a lie.

I had no idea what I thought, so how could you?

eleven

I ran all the way home. I couldn't tell you how long it took, or even the names of the streets I ran down. Pushing open the door, I walked in, dropping my shoes to the floor and leaning heavily against the door to close it.

"Soph?" My father grunted as he hoisted himself out of the chair. "Soph is that you?"

Questions. So many questions with no answers. My phone vibrated. It was you again. Thirteen missed calls. Countless texts begging for me to let you explain. And you could have. In a message, in a text, but you didn't. You only pleaded for me to talk to you, to pick up the phone, to listen.

My mind was a mess. Thoughts, questions and answers tumbled about my brain, tripping, stumbling and rolling over each other until I was unable to follow a single line of thought. But there was only one question that remained. Only one that I could focus on.

Why?

"Yeah, Dad." I rubbed the lipstick off my mouth, swiped the mascara stains from under my eyes and took a deep breath before stepping into the lounge.

He blinked in surprise. "Why are you wearing a sheet?"

Striding past him, I avoided meeting his eye. "I just need a moment alone."

"Are you okay?" he called as the door shut.

Did you know who I was from the start?

Why did you let me pour out my heart and my soul and not utter a word?

Was this just some sick game you wanted to play?

Did you see her that night?

Were you a witness to your father's guilt?

I let the sheet drop to the floor and hurriedly drew my dressing gown around my shoulders, pulling it tight around my neck just as Dad knocked.

I flashed him a smile as I opened the door and assured him I was fine. With painful movements he lowered himself back into his chair. He had enough to worry about.

"Have you had something to eat?" I asked.

He waved aside my concern but still stared at me curiously. "I heated one of those dinners in the microwave." Reaching over the side of his chair, he took another sip of the dark liquid in his glass. "We need to talk."

I hardly heard his words because I was too busy thinking about you.

Was it bad that I still lusted after you? Was it bad that I wanted to run to you? That I longed for that swell of denial and excess, restriction and freedom that all rolled into that one night with you?

I needed to get away from Dad's imploring eyes. "Not now, Dad. I think I'm just going to call it a night."

Dad grinned up at me, nostalgia for an often used joke. "I think it's always been called that."

I couldn't smile. I couldn't laugh.

Dad's expression dropped. "We need to talk, Soph. The police called."

"Why?"

"They've got the results of the autopsy and someone has come forward with new information."

My heart jumped. "And you went without me?"

"I was right all along, Soph." Dad's face gleamed. He sat forward on the edge of his chair, eager to share the information. "They know who did it." His eyes were fire. "I knew it. I knew it all along," he muttered. "The police always insisted that they looked into him and he was clean as a whistle, but I knew. No one is that clean. It was just fucking deep pockets. They strangled her, Soph. Those fucking bastards strangled her and then hid the body. They paid people off to keep it a secret but this guy that came forward said he couldn't stand the guilt anymore. He saw it. He saw everything."

Nausea tumbled in my gut. I struggled to smile but smile I did because I knew he drew strength from it. It made him think I was okay. Everything was okay.

He relayed the story with sadness and strength. He told

me of the last moments of my sister's life. And with each word that came from his mouth, the sky began to fall.

She danced. People were transfixed. Alcohol was poured, music floated through the air, and the crowd urged her on. She had one drink afterwards, maybe two. The witness didn't want to come forward but the revival of her case in the news brought along guilt he thought he had long buried.

He was the one who had bound her hands and her feet. He was the one who stuffed her broken body into the back of the stolen car. He was the one who drove her to the water.

But he was not her killer.

In the story he told, the killer was you.

He told of an only child of a wealthy family, spoilt and favoured since birth. He told the story of a child who was used to getting what he wanted. Of a child who was never told no.

He told of how he wanted her and how she said no.

Of seeing him wrestle with her, drag her into a room by the pull of her hair. He told of her muffled cries and of her silence.

And then he told of seeing her afterwards, the marks and the bruises. The red welts around her neck. Her limp and lifeless body.

He told of the money your family paid for his silence. He spoke of loyalty but he also spoke of truth.

Dad's eyes danced as he told me. He was no longer in

limbo, waiting for my sister to walk back through the door. There was passion in his stance. Life in his movements. There was now something driving him.

Revenge.

You.

I didn't say anything while he spoke, because what could I say?

"You see?" Dad said. "I was right about them being responsible, but I was wrong about who. It was the son. The father was merely the one to cover it up. The police are waiting on the arrest warrant now. They are going to bring these bastards down."

My muttered response must have satisfied him as he sat back in his chair, nodding to himself and I returned to my room. But once I closed the door, I bolted across the space, heaving into the bin beside my bed and emptying the contents of my stomach. My hands flew to my neck as if somehow, if I covered my bruises, covered the evidence of you, this nightmare would end.

But it didn't.

Through the closed door of my bedroom, I could still hear the low hum of the voices of the television. I had fallen asleep to that noise almost every night for years. It was a comfort. But now the muted voices only served to taunt me. Tearing my gown from my body, I threw it to the floor and stood in front of the mirror. I stared at myself as I ran my fingers over my body, starting with the darkening marks on my neck. The marks left by you. Thoughts of you, of my sister, of our time together, swirled until I no longer knew what was truth and what was fiction.

I thought of you.

I thought of your lips, so red, so sensual as they pressed against my skin. I thought of your eyes, so piercing, so pure, like they could see into my soul. I thought of your hair and the dark tufts trapped between my fingers.

I thought of your hands wrapped around my throat, and the vision blurred and twisted in my mind until my sister and I became one and when you killed her you killed me.

Twenty-three missed calls. You were relentless. My voicemail was filled with the sound of you. I heard your inhales and exhales as you sucked on poison. You claimed your innocence. You denied knowing who I was. Whose sister I was. And I was ashamed to admit there was a part of me that wanted to believe you.

I couldn't talk because I didn't know what to say. I couldn't listen to your voice, not knowing if it were truth or lies. So I hid under the protection of a blanket.

It was only when silence came that I could piece together the thoughts in my brain.

I knew what I must do.

The police were coming for you.

But I wanted to get there first.

twelve

When I snuck out of the house, Dad wasn't in his chair. It was the first time in a long time that he actually went to bed. The streets were deserted as the pizza shop and its neon sign came into view.

"Hey, babe. I don't think you're on tonight." Caleb met me at the back door. The smell of dough and grease floated in the air. He looked me up and down. "You look like shit, by the way."

I folded my arms across my chest, staring up at him, chewing the lip caught between my teeth.

Caleb looked at me curiously. "You coming in or what?"

"I need something." I looked about, waiting for the boss, another workmate, someone or anyone to appear.

Caleb frowned. "What sort of something?"

"Something to relax."

He narrowed his eyes. "Mind or body?"

"Body."

"Like muscle relaxants?"

"Something stronger."

Caleb shifted uncomfortably. "I think you need to tell me what they are for." His eyes darted back inside the shop and he moved down a step. "Who they are for."

I took a deep breath. "I just need someone to understand what it feels like to be powerless."

Caleb grinned and ran his tongue over his teeth. "And this person who needs to understand this, is this because of something he did, assuming it's a he?"

I nodded. There was little more else I could do. My body was trembling and I shoved my hands further under my armpits, shielding them from Caleb.

"Meet me after my shift."

"You haven't got anything now?"

Caleb scoffed. "I'm not a walking pharmacy."

I chewed so hard on my bottom lip it bled. "I need it now."

Caleb chuckled. "Fine. Fine. I'm sure I can scrounge something up. Wait here." He disappeared and I stood on the street as fat drops of rain fell from the sky.

"Here." He deposited a few pills into my hand. "That's all I've got on me. It's just benzo but an overdose should do the job. How big is he?"

I looked Caleb over, noting that he was around the same build as you. "About your size."

Caleb chewed on his lip, calculating in his mind. He took a pill out of my hand, paused, then placed it back and shrugged. "Should be enough."

"Thanks." I shoved them into my pocket, hoping they would be enough to do the job. I started to walk away but Caleb's voice pulled me back.

"Is everything okay, Soph? Do you need company on this little vigilante mission?"

I forced a smile, walking backwards so I could face him while escaping him. "Don't worry. It's nothing."

Because you were.

As I walked the streets you called again and this time I answered.

"Hi." My voice was timid. Cautious.

"Thank god." Your words came out in a gush of relief. "I need to explain. You have to listen to me."

"I'm listening." I would let you talk. It worked in my favour. You had no idea I was aware of what you had done.

"It's not what you think," you started.

I had promised myself to let you talk, but words flew out of my mouth before I could stop them. "And what is it you think that I think?" I was sharp. Blunt. You thought your only fault was being their son.

"That I hid who I was. I need to see you, explain in person."

I wondered then if you knew how easy you made it. How desperate you sounded.

"Fine."

"Fine?" You repeated the word. "Come over to my place."

"No. Meet me by the estuary."

"The estuary?"

Just like the alarm bells that should have sounded when you knew my surname without introduction, or when you sent a car to my place without an address, you ignored the warning bells that should have sounded in your head.

You should have known.

I named the time and you agreed.

You shouldn't have.

thirteen

Before I left, I wrote my father a note. It told the truth about everything. About you and about me. It told him where I would be. What I was about to do.

I took a taxi to the estuary and got there before you did. The sun was just beginning to set and it cast orange and red and yellow over the water. You were too good for such beauty but I needed there to be poetry in my actions. I needed you to feel what she felt. What I felt.

I sat on the wooden bench and waited. In my hands was a cup of coffee. In my pocket were headphones. Another cup sat on the seat beside me.

You walked with your head lowered to the ground. I swallowed the knot in my throat, denying the feelings of love and lust that swirled through me at the sight of you. You had fooled me. Made a mockery of my family.

You would pay.

You didn't say anything as you approached, just sat beside me. I slid the coffee towards you and you took it without hesitation, the scent of alcohol on your breath. You believed in my innocence, my naivety.

You didn't know me.

"I'm sorry." That was what you said when you came inside me too. "I had no idea who you were when I met you." That was a lie. "I had no idea that you were Phoebe's sister."

You said her name so easily. It should have burned your throat. It should have ripped open the flesh of your lips and welded your teeth shut.

You took a sip of your coffee and shuddered at its bitterness. "And when I did find out, I didn't want to tell you who I was. I was already falling for you, Sophie. I was already in love."

I wanted to scream. I wanted to yell your lies into the cool air of the evening. But instead, all I did was raise my drink to my mouth which prompted you to do the same. I watched your fingers and imagined them wrapped around the neck of my sister as she pleaded for you to stop.

Did her voice sound just like mine?

Your free hand, the one without the coffee, was stuffed into your pockets, fumbling with something. For a brief moment I wondered if it was wrapped around the same thing as mine. Something smooth and fine. Something that would cut the air from your throat.

"Do you believe me?" You appeared so honest in your plea, and for a moment, I let myself consider what would happen if I said yes.

Would you take me in your arms?

Would you press your lips against mine?

Would I end up like my sister?

I shifted closer, disarming you with my boldness. "Tell me about her."

"About who?" Confusion passed over your features and for a moment I hesitated.

What if I was wrong? What if what the witness had said was lies?

You shook your head.

"About who?" you asked again.

"About my sister." I said it so quietly the words were almost carried away by the wind, but your beautiful eyes narrowed ever so slightly.

"What do you mean? I never knew her." You opened and closed your fingers around the cup of coffee, testing their strength. The police had told my father it took a lot of force to strangle someone long enough for them to die. And your strength was fading.

I needed to keep you talking, allow enough time for the drugs to start to work. "Don't lie to me," I warned.

You attempted to look at me with wide and innocent eyes, but as soon as you met my gaze, you knew that I knew the truth.

"What have you done?" You moved your fingers again. They moved slowly. They lacked strength. Your breathing slowed.

I smiled and leaned closer. "When she was begging for

you to stop, did you listen or did you simply tighten your fingers?"

Even when confronted with the truth you insisted on proclaiming your innocence. "It was a mistake. I didn't mean too… I took things too far. I loved her."

"You didn't even know her!" I spat. "Did she claw at your hands like I did? Did she draw blood with her nails?"

You blinked but you didn't move away. "She agreed."

I laughed then. "She agreed to let you kill her?"

Something about your expression changed. Your features twisted and darkened. "She agreed to let me strangle her. I paid her. She said yes." The coffee cup fell from your hands and I thought that meant your strength was gone. I was wrong. "You look so much like her. Especially when you posed for me. She posed for me too, just like you did. The same stance and everything. Only I didn't have to pay you for it. I guess in the end, I didn't pay her either."

That was what made me snap. I stood, just as you lurched towards me, pulling the cord of my headphones out of my pocket and moving behind you. But you were too slow. Your limbs moved as though through thick liquid. Your arms flailed behind you, reaching for me as I looped the cord around your neck and pulled tight.

"Do you think she felt helpless under your hands?" I hissed in his ear. "Do you feel helpless under mine?"

I think you tried to laugh, but it came out as nothing more than a gurgle. Your hands clawed at your throat, trying desperately to get under the tension of the cord. Tossing your body left and right, you tried to throw me off balance, but the drugs had made you slow and your movements laboured. I increased my grip, jerking the cord tighter, pulling harder. It cut into my fingers but I didn't care.

Lowering my mouth to your ear, I let my lips brush over your skin. "I hope you're thinking of her now. Of what you did. That is why you're here. This is your fault. You did this. You ruined me."

I wanted there to be a symmetry to your death. For you to die by my hand in the same manner as she had died by yours.

Giving up on releasing the cord, you fumbled through the pockets of your jacket. I didn't see exactly what you pulled out but it glinted in the setting sun. I tried to move, but it was too late. Your flailing dug the knife into my side and I cried out in pain, releasing the cord.

You coughed, drawing air into your desperate lungs as I fell to the ground, clutching at my side.

"You bitch!" Your voice was different than before. You lunged at me but I jerked my body away, dragging it through the dirt and the stones of the path. Even though your movements were stilted by chemicals, mine were stilted by pain.

"What makes you think she wanted me to stop?" Spit flew from your mouth. "What makes you think she didn't enjoy it, just like you did?" Your smile was cold and cruel.

Blood seeped through my clothing and onto the ground. I

tried to stand but ended up falling. You threw your body onto mine, weighing me down, pressing me into the stones.

You hissed words in my ear. Dark words. Filthy words. I rammed my elbow into your face and you reeled back as blood gushed from your nostrils.

Fear pulsed. This wasn't what was supposed to happen. You were supposed to be the one on the ground. You were supposed to be the one suffering. My fingers clawed the dirt as I dragged my broken and bleeding body away from you. But you came after me, stumbling, barely able to keep on your feet. The ground gave way beneath me and I rolled into a ditch, grass scratching at my skin, tickling the tip of my nose as tears streamed down my cheeks.

You lurched after me, leaning down to press your face into mine. "Why did you have to do this?" Your eyes were dark with desire. You almost looked at me lovingly as I lay there, the sky darkening above me. "We could have had something. You were my second chance. You were like me. You were dark. You craved pain with your pleasure, I saw it in your eyes. I knew it by the way your body responded."

The blade glinted in the light of the setting sun once again as you reached out. And even though your movements were slow, I still didn't know what you had done until I felt the warmth and the wet on my neck. I lifted trembling hands and they came away red. I tried to talk but it felt as though I was drowning. Nothing came out but gurgles and gasps.

You stroked my cheek with a cold and clammy hand and

hushed my desperate babble. "It's okay." With concentrated effort, you reached into your pockets and pulled out a packet of cigarettes. Your hands trembled. Your eyes danced. You lit the end of a cigarette and let the first plume of smoke into the air.

"I lied." Honesty came from you now that you thought this was the end. You took another drag on the cigarette and winked, only it came out slow and over-exaggerated. "I knew who you were the moment I met you. I knew whose sister you were."

I didn't feel any pain. I only felt cold. Blood bubbled in my throat as I attempted to gasp for air, and panic made my heart thud.

You dragged yourself back up the bank of the ditch, distancing yourself from me but still watching as my life dripped away.

"You look so much like her, but I guess you know that. I just couldn't help myself. I had to have you like I had her." You took another drag on the cigarette as though my life wasn't draining away, as though we had all the time in the world. "It was the first time I tried it. I didn't know how to control myself. I took it too far." You shrugged your shoulders as you said it, as though it was nothing more than a simple mistake, a slip of the hand. "I didn't mean to, if that makes you feel any better. But she was just so beautiful as she struggled. I wanted to watch. I needed to watch. I'd seen her so many times at my father's parties. She was there to entertain the men, I knew that but I didn't care. When she danced there was nothing more beautiful in the world. I had to have her. Of course," you chuckled, "she didn't agree. She dismissed me, looked at me with disdain." You took another inhale of smoke and blew it over me as I spluttered and choked on my own blood, lying discarded in the ditch.

"You know they won't get me, don't you? My father will make sure if that. He knows it was just a mistake. I'm not a killer."

I wondered if you knew how demented you sounded. I wondered how I had not seen it before. I struggled to speak and you leaned forward as though attempting to listen to me.

"I should probably go." As you got to your feet, you swayed, holding out your hands in an effort to steady your body, your breath coming out labored and forced. The outline of your cock was visible through your pants. You were hard as you watched me bleed in the ditch. Throwing the butt of your cigarette into the water, you looked at me once more. "Don't worry, it won't be much longer and then it will all be over. You'll get to see your sister again." You winked. "Say hi from me."

I could only see bits of you through the blades of the grass. I was hidden. Only whispers of air reached my lungs and they were wet with blood.

You blew me a kiss and turned, but when you did, your body jerked backwards and you fell to the ground with a thud. Surprise flashed in your eyes as the silhouette of my father appeared on the horizon. You hadn't counted on him being here. You hadn't counted on him bringing a weapon. You twisted and thrashed but your poisoned body was no match for a bullet. I tried to smile at you through the blades of grass but I don't know if I succeeded. All I know is that your eyes searched out mine in terror. You coughed and your body convulsed. Blood spluttered from lips tainted with blue and trickled down your chin.

My father stumbled through the grass, wild eyes searching the surroundings. "Sophie!" he called out in desperation. "Sophie!"

I tried to answer but nothing came. Not even a gurgle. There was no warmth left in me. Even the blood soaking my neck was now cold. It gathered in the dip between my collarbones.

"Sophie!" Dad called again, running and stumbling away from me. I tried to lift my hand but there was nothing left. Panic ricocheted as the blood rose up my throat, suffocating me.

Dad's voice carried my name on the breeze, louder than it was before. My heart swelled with the hope that he might find me before there was nothing left.

Your lifeless eyes stared back at me, red veins dancing over the white.

Even then my heart cried for you.

* * *

They told me I was lucky. Lucky you didn't cut any deeper. Lucky my dad found me when he did. Lucky the ambulance came so quickly.

But they didn't know the truth. They didn't know that part of me wished I had died with you. It would have been a kindness. By getting vengeance on you, I had become you. Capable of killing. Capable of death. If you hadn't had that knife, I would have been the one to end your life. It would have been me in jail awaiting trial instead of my father. It was what I deserved.

It was three days before they allowed me to remove the bandage and see the scar you left me with. The nurses told me it would fade, but I didn't want it to. I want it to stay angry and raw and red. I want it there because it reminds me of you and everything you took from me.

But even though you took everything, even though you ruined me, my heart still flutters when I think of you. Maybe you are right. Maybe we are the same.

Just look at me now in this world without you.

I have nothing.

But I am still here.

And you are not.

About the Author

Facebook Reader Group:

www.facebook.com/groups/sabrerose

Newsletter:

www.subscribepage.com/sabreroseauthor

Social Media:

www.facebook.com/sabreroseauthor

www.twitter.com/sabreroseauthor

Website:

www.sabreroseauthor.com

Email:

sabreroseauthor@gmail.com

Books by Sabre Rose

Contemporary Romance

THORNTON BROTHERS

This steamy contemporary romance series follows the lives of the Thornton Brothers as told by the women who love them.

TOUCHED

TEMPTED

TAKEN

TORN

*

TEARS

*

TORMENT

TURMOIL

Psychological Romantic Suspense

SAY YOU LOVE ME

Dark Romance

REQUESTED TRILOGY

For lovers of dark romance, the Requested Trilogy is an enthralling, twisted and disturbingly beautiful story of a girl taken captive.

DON'T SAY A WORD
UNTIL YOU'RE MINE
MY SWEET SONGBIRD

BLACK SWAN TRILOGY

A dark romance set in the same world as the Requested Trilogy, this is a compelling story of a girl who struggles with being known as the daughter of a monster.

DAUGHTER OF A MONSTER
SEARCHING FOR HOPE
AMONG THE SINS OF MY FATHER

Printed in Great Britain
by Amazon